The Belt, the Balloon, the Flowers

The Belt, the Balloon, the Flowers

A Christmas Story

Chad R. Allen

For Dad

Be kind, for everyone you meet
is fighting a hard battle.

—Ian MacLaren

"Well, crap."

Jim kept staring at his belt buckle. The metal piece that was supposed to go through the holes had just snapped, and he was trying to figure out some way to make it work. No use.

Jim rolled the belt up and placed it on his dresser, his mind slipping back to Italy twenty-five years earlier. He was there as part of a Rotary-sponsored cultural exchange for young professionals. A great opportunity, tainted by what Jim hated to admit felt like the unraveling of his romance back home.

He and his girlfriend, Emily, agreed the month apart would be a good test for their relationship—he hoped his absence would make her heart grow fonder.

One afternoon in Florence, when his group had some free time, Jim tried calling Emily despite the expense, but she didn't answer. He tried again—multiple times—with no answer. Sighing, Jim pocketed his phone and stepped into the lively streets.

The surrounding buildings drew his eyes upward. The architecture was so foreign and soaring and elegant. Was it any wonder some of the world's finest artists had a connection to this place? He wished Emily could be there with him.

Glancing down at the cobblestone road, Jim noticed his empty belt loops. He'd meant to buy a new belt before leaving the States but ran out of time. A few blocks later he spotted one—a brown leather strap with a silver buckle—hanging from a street vendor's cart. Jim wasn't in the mood to try his broken Italian, but asked with hand gestures if he could try it on. It fit.

"Ah! It looks-a good on you," the kind vendor said.

Something about the contrast between Emily's unresponsiveness and this old man's gentle face and ability to speak English brought a lump to Jim's throat. The man saw Jim's emotion and must have felt sorry for him. "You keep it, you keep. No charge," he said. Jim held up his hands in protest, but the man insisted.

"No problem-o! It's yours!" he said. "Tink nice tings about Italia!"

Wrapped in his first souvenir, Jim wandered the grand halls of the Uffizi. Marveled at Michelangelo's ghostly incomplete sculptures. Stared into the eyes of Venus floating above Botticelli's clamshell.

When he got home from the trip, Emily was not at the airport to welcome him.

These memories all came rushing back as he stood there in his bedroom. Jim realized this was more than just a belt to him. It was a symbol of that rich, painful time in Italy. Like a memento and a scar in one.

He pulled up the shade. It was snowing steadily, the first good snow of the season, and he paused to take it in. Jim loved this time of year. As he watched the large flakes blanketing three bushes in his backyard, they briefly became the three magi on their long journey to Bethlehem.

Jim Maloney was now a 48-year-old car salesman at Petersen Toyota. Just last week he'd eaten a piece of cake at the 20-year anniversary party his coworkers threw for him and a technician who'd also been there that long.

As he continued getting ready for work without his belt, Jim wondered if leather repair was still a thing. It seemed ancient—like woodworking or illuminating manuscripts.

While eating his cereal he looked up "leather repair near me," and sure enough a couple of places came up, one of which, Dan's Leather Repair, was just 4.2 miles from his house. He decided to swing by on his lunch break.

A bell rang as he entered, and he closed the door fast to keep out the cold. The smell of the place was the first thing he noticed. A mix of shoe polish and…was that vinegar? Pungent but not entirely unpleasant.

He also noticed some forgotten shoes in the entryway. A pair of men's dress shoes. Converse high-tops. A pair of high heels.

He wondered about their erstwhile owners; images flashed in his mind. A businessman rushing through an airport. A high school kid swishing a jump shot. A lady whirling under a glittering chandelier.

From the looks of things, none of them was coming back to claim their shoes anytime soon.

Jim stepped to the counter and waited. Behind the counter was a wall with a doorway through which he saw tools neatly hanging above a workbench. Then a man appeared.

"Good morning." The voice was weathered.

"Morning!"

Jim waited for the usual "How can I help you?" but it never came. The man just stood there looking at him, arms in an upside-down V as he leaned against the counter. *This must be Dan.*

Dan was average height, in his sixties, slightly creased face, with a straw-colored wispy cloud for hair. *Robert Redfordish*, Jim thought—*well, the hair at least.*

"Um. Well, I have this belt. Have had for a long time, but this morning, *this* broke." Jim showed the broken tongue to Dan. "Is there anything you can do for that?"

Dan took the belt and buckle into his hands, turning it over with his darkened fingers.

"Hm, you need a new buckle."

"I see. Can you find one that will work?"

Dan looked up. "Does it need to match this one exactly?" He asked as though he'd received complaints in the past from those who had expected a perfect match.

"No, no. I mean, something close would be great, but it doesn't need to be exact."

"OK." Dan was already bent over, writing out a work order. He ripped off the claim ticket, held it out to Jim.

"Should be about $15. Give me a week."

"Wow, that's great," Jim said, not expecting this to be so easy. Then he decided to share more. "This belt actually means a lot to me. Picked it up in Italy a long time ago." As he looked at Dan, Jim realized he was hoping for some reassurance his belt was in good hands.

Then Jim realized something else. Dan looked sad. Something about his expression went beyond simple fatigue. What was his story? Jim searched for an image in his mind—none came.

Sadness. That's what Jim saw.

"Well," Dan said, "give me a week."

Jim sat in his car, letting it warm up. He had a strong feeling this repairman had been through something, and he wondered if he could help.

Inside the shop, Dan cut the stitching that held the broken buckle, and set it aside. He attached the work order to the empty strap and hung it on the rack beside two others, where it would stay until the new buckle arrived. He chucked the broken buckle in the trash can and winced at the clatter.

A framed photo of his wife, Sarah, leaned against a jar of brushes on the workbench.

⌗

A week later Dan's phone rang. It was Jim.

"Hey there, Jim Maloney here. I brought my belt in about a week ago."

"Mhm, just got the new buckle. Should be finished with it later this morning."

"Terrific! I'll stop by this afternoon to pick it up."

It looked better than new, Jim thought, as he ran his forefinger over the smooth, shiny metal. Way shinier than before.

"Wow, I guess I didn't realize how beat-up the original was. This looks great. How much do I owe you?"

"$13," Dan said.

Jim looked in his wallet and saw a ten and a five. "Well, here, take $15."

"You sure? I have change."

"I'm sure, the belt looks great—I'm grateful. Thank you."

"You're welcome." Dan reached down to pick up a paperclip from the floor. Threw it into a magnetic tray.

He looks sad.

"Hey,…take care," Jim said.

Dan looked at Jim, then down, and walked back into his shop.

Jim was even more certain this guy had something going on in his life, but what could he do? *Buy him flowers? Buy flowers for a complete stranger? That's just weird.*

Lately Petersen Toyota was short on new inventory, so Jim spent a lot of time looking for good used cars to roll into their lot. Folks looking to trade in and trade up.

He was writing a thank-you card to a customer who recently purchased a van from him—something his manager taught him years before. It was a small gesture that came with the possibility of new business, both from referrals and from the same customer later.

As he signed the card, he thought about writing one for Dan. *That wouldn't be too strange, would it? A simple thank-you card?*

All his thank-you cards at work were emblazoned with the Toyota logo, but when he got home, he pulled out a card with a navy blue cursive *Thanks!* on the front.

Dear Dan,

Thank you for fixing my belt. It was probably just a simple job for you, but the belt means a lot to me, and I can't thank you enough for giving it new life.

"New life?" Jim muttered. "A bit much."

But he wasn't going to throw it away and start a new one.

Sincerely,

Jim

On his way into work, he drove by the shop and dropped it through the mail slot in the front door.

When Dan arrived, two of the four pieces of mail he saw were advertisements—one for an upcoming mattress sale, "Buy One, Get One Free!" and another for a "$12.99 Pizza and Hot Wings Deal!!!" The third was his heating bill, which he was not looking forward to opening. And the fourth was unusual. It did not have his address on the front—just "Dan."

He opened the envelope and read the card from Jim. A moment later the card was sitting next to the sender's broken buckle in the trash.

———

That night, Jim prepped dinner with his wife, Anne, while their two teenagers watched videos in their bedrooms. "So, I got my belt fixed."

"That's great, who did it?"

"Little shop down on Maryland. Dan's Leather Repair."

"Great, was it expensive?"

"Nah, $15. But the guy there—Dan, I guess. He seems really sad."

"Oh?"

"Yeah, like…I just feel bad for him."

———

A week later, Jim was at the dollar store picking up birthday plates and plasticware for his daughter's upcoming sleepover party.

As he waited in line, his eyes drifted over to the balloon counter. A heavyset lady was handing a newly inflated "Happy Birthday" to a woman in a soft pink coat, and just above their heads was a flattened "Thank You" balloon hanging on the wall. Bright red, silver cursive lettering. *Christmasy*, he thought.

When the cashier asked him "Is that everything?" he surprised himself and said, "No, I'd also like that thank-you balloon up there, the red one."

"No problem."

As he shuffled back to his car, the balloon pelting his face, he felt silly. *What the hell am I doing? Why do I care?* He wasn't sure. He just did. Maybe he saw something of the repairman in himself, like if his life had been just a few clicks different, he'd end up feeling as sad as he imagined Dan was.

The next morning, as he neared the shop, he really hoped Dan wouldn't be in, and he wasn't. Jim's watch read 8:07, and the shop didn't open until 9:00. He slipped off his gloves, tied the balloon securely to the door handle, and left.

Pulling into the lot a half hour later, Dan's first thought was some punk kids were pranking him. But when he approached and saw the words "Thank You" in a cursive font, his fear turned to under-his-breath disgust. "What a waste, now I gotta mess with this." He had no idea who it was from.

He went inside, retrieved a pair of scissors, cut the ribbon off the handle, and walked back in. He looked at the balloon and for a moment thought about tying it to the coat tree. He even held it there to see what it would look like. He decided it looked dumb, stabbed the balloon, and threw it away.

Wait, he thought. *That belt guy?*

Later in the week Jim was at the grocery store grabbing a sandwich and a few other things. The Maloney kitchen was out of fruit and granola bars—two staples for the kids' lunches.

On his way to the register, he saw a sign in the floral department—

Beautiful Bouquets
$9.99

No, he thought. *No, you wouldn't…*

At this point Jim was frustrated with himself. *I've already given him a card and a balloon! Why do I need to buy him flowers?!*

"Because he's hurting." That's what Jim heard back. "He's hurting."

Fine. He picked up one of the bouquets and scanned it along with a deli sandwich, a bag of clementines, some strawberries, and a box of peanut butter–flavored granola bars.

This time, as he pulled into the parking lot, he realized with a start he would not be able to do this anonymously. Or at least not easily. He couldn't just leave the flowers on the ground in front of the door. Maybe he could walk in quickly, set them on the counter, and leave.

That's it. That's what he'd do. They could just be anonymous.

He tried to ease the door open without making a sound, but it was impossible. The door wouldn't budge without a solid push, which made the bell ring out for the whole damn world to hear.

Never mind. He moved swiftly and placed the flowers on the counter.

As he turned to leave, Dan walked in and saw the flowers.

"Oh. Uh. Hi," said Jim.

"Morning."

"Um, my wife thought—it's just that. Listen, I—. It's just that you seemed like you might need a little encouragement, and…I want you to have these."

For a moment Dan just stood there. Eventually he picked up the flowers and looked at them. He looked at Jim.

"Thank you, I—" It seemed like he was going to say "I appreciate it," but he stuffed that down and said "thank you" again.

"You're welcome. Take care."

And Jim left. Quickly.

That was about as awkward as it gets, he thought to himself.

Dan turned and brought the flowers into the shop. He tossed them into the trash, where they lay with, among other things, a broken buckle, a thank-you card, and the remains of a mylar balloon.

Then he looked at the picture on his workbench. Sarah's eyes were radiant as ever.

He started to cry. This time, he decided, he wasn't going to hold back. He let the emotion beat against his chest. He let the tears and the snot and the sobbing—he let it all come.

"I miss you," he whispered.

As he blinked, he saw the flowers. He picked them up and placed them in a fast-food cup from lunch the day before.

Dan looked at the flowers next to the face of the woman who meant the world to him.

They seemed to belong there.

Author's Note

The original idea for this story came from real life. Much of it is pure imagination, but it did develop out of actual events. I recall sharing the story idea with my daughter. At that point the idea was in the form of a silent film, where the characters' actions alone would carry the story forward. I can still visualize Jim's flashback to Italy and the jovial street vendor, then the flash forward to his bedroom, holding the broken belt. And of course, there are a lot of visual possibilities for the thank-you card, the balloon, the flowers, the photograph of Sarah.

The idea also came to me with a soundtrack. It was a song I'd heard, but I couldn't remember when or where. I certainly had no idea who the recording artist was. I scoured my Spotify history searching for it to no avail. But one day, in Chicago to support my friend Alice who was running the marathon there, I went to a coffee shop to do my Morning Pages. I often listen to instrumental music when writing, and for some reason that day I picked a playlist I hadn't played in a while, "Yoga Soft & Gentle." Imagine how excited I was when, about ten tracks in, the song came on! I'm very happy to share that the song is "Bluebird" by Alexis Ffrench. If you're inclined to read the story again, it might be fun to play this song in the background.

I happen to be writing and publishing this story as AI Large Language Models are becoming widely available. I used one of these, ChatGPT, to play around with a cover image. I recognize that using AI-generated art can be controversial, but I decided it was the right pick for this project. I also asked AI to imagine that Jim and Dan became friends after this story. What might they look like standing beside each other? Voila!

I come away from having written this little story with immense respect and admira-
tion for fiction writers. Casting a spell with
words so effectively that readers can get lost
in a book—that is not easy! The least we can
do for the novelists we love is post a review!
(Oh, and if you'd be willing to post one for

"The Belt, the Balloon, the Flowers," I'd be beyond grateful!)

Finally, I just want to say thank you for not only reading my story, but now all the way to the end of this author's note. I'm grateful. This foray into fiction has been a lot of fun. I don't know if I'll write more fiction, but I do have some ideas in the wings…

Acknowledgments

I'm grateful to the people who helped bring this little story into being.

To my wife, Alyssa, and to our kids, Claire and Lucas—you're the inspiration behind everything I do. Alyssa, thank you for being the very first person to hear this story, patiently listening as I read it aloud in our living room.

To the BookCamp community—thank you for gathering with me beside the fire at BookCamp Live 2025 and listening so generously to an early draft. Your encouragement that night is the reason this story made its way into the world.

To the readers on my email list—your feedback on the cover, your responses, and your steady support over the years have been the backbone of my work. You're why I was able to step out on my own nearly eight years ago, and I'm deeply grateful.

Thanks as well to my friends and neighbors—Mike, Alice, Peter, Annette, Nate, Steve, Andy, Orly, Melissa, Clare, Russ, and Patty—for thoughtful feedback and gentle nudges that helped this piece find its shape.

Thanks too to the fellas I've been having breakfast with nearly every Friday morning for who knows how many years. You've taught me so much about how guys can show up for one another.

Special thanks to Chuck, who suggested making the balloon on the cover red for a more Christmasy touch. (It was green once upon a time—on the cover and in the story.)

Chad R. Allen is a writer, editor, and writing coach with more than twenty-five years in publishing. His work has been featured in *Lifehacker*, Jane Friedman's blog, and *The Good Men Project*. He leads BookCamp, an online community and training center for writers, and is the author of *Do Your Art*. Chad lives in Michigan, with his wife, Alyssa, and their two children. For more about Chad and his work, visit www.chadrallen.com.

Also from Chad R. Allen

Available Wherever Books Are Sold